MENACE
WORLD BOOK DAY

Written by
Steven Butler

Illustrated by Steve May

PUFFIN

PUFFIN BOOKS

UK | USA | Canada | Ireland | Australia
India | New Zealand | South Africa

Puffin Books is part of the Penguin Random House group of companies
whose addresses can be found at global.penguinrandomhouse.com.

puffinbooks.com

Penguin
Random House
UK

First published 2015
001

Written by Steven Butler
Illustrated by Steve May
Copyright © DC Thomson & Co. Ltd, 2015
The Beano ® ©, Dennis the Menace ® © and associated
characters are TM and © DC Thomson & Co. Ltd 2015
All rights reserved

The moral right of the author, illustrator
and copyright holders has been asserted

Set in Soupbone
Printed in Great Britain by Clays Ltd, St Ives plc

A CIP catalogue record for this book is available from the British Library

ISBN: 978–0–141–35869–7

www.greenpenguin.co.uk

MIX
Paper from
responsible sources
FSC® C018179

Penguin Random House is committed to a
sustainable future for our business, our readers
and our planet. This book is made from Forest
Stewardship Council® certified paper.

For my niece,

and all those years of

menacing yet to come

BRRRRP!

Tomorrow is World

WHAT

Day!?!?

B-

Bo-

Boo-

BOOK!?!?!?!?!

1

WORLD BOOK DAY!?!?

AGAIN??

Has everyone completely lost their minds? Have they gone crackers? Did the planet spin too fast and everyone's brains were whisked into bonkers-booky-porridge?

Why isn't it WORLD ICE-CREAM DAY?

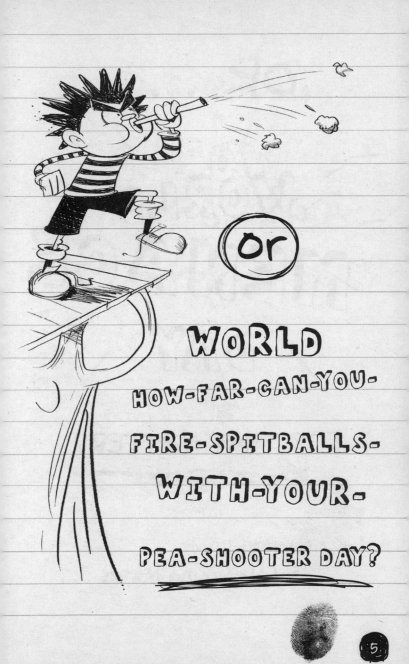

or

WORLD

HOW-FAR-CAN-YOU-

FIRE-SPITBALLS-

WITH-YOUR-

PEA-SHOOTER DAY?

OR . . .

WORLD MENACE DAY

FOR THAT MATTER?

We're in serious trouble,

my Menacing Mates . . .

It's not that ALL books are bad. Some books are **COMPLETELY MEGA BRILLIANT!!** My favourite book, Mutant Cannibal-Zombies Ate My Homework, is probably the best book that has ever been written.

It's <u>TERRIFIC!</u> I found it at the back of Beanotown Library when we went there on a school trip. I had wandered off in fear that I was only seconds away from certain death because of BOREDOM-BRAIN-ROT when I spotted it . . . It was on a shelf with a sign that said

MUTANT CANNIBAL ZOMBIES ATE MY HOMEWORK! BEVEN STUTLER

'SCARY! NOT FOR CHILDREN!'

Not for children?

NOT FOR CHILDREN?

It should have said . . .

NOT FOR SOFTIES!

The books on that shelf were

MENACING MASTERPIECES!

There was . . .

PSYCHO
LIBRARIANS:
They'll Shush You
to Death!

ATTACK OF THE
70-FOOT
BOTTOM!

GUINEA
PIGS
From Beyond
the Grave

KILLERSAURUS
REX
RETURNS!!

It was the first time in my life I ever realized that books could be fun. Before that, I always thought they were invented by grown-ups just to put children to sleep at night.

Those **AMAZING** books aren't what's bothering me, though. The problem is we NEVER get to read any stories like that. Last World Book Day, Headmaster sat us all down in assembly and read *Mrs Twinkle's Magical Bunny Circus* to us . . . **TWICE!** It was torture . . . **TORURE**!!! All those skipping, twirling bunnies with their magic puppy and kitten pals made me feel sick for days. But you can guess who loved it . . .

Walter!

My archest enemy in the whole world.

Walter always wins the 'Top Reader' badge every term. **<u>EVERY TERM</u>!!!** My teacher, Mrs Creecher, and Headmaster think Walter is BRILLIANT because he's the most BUM-FACIEST of all the pupils at Bash Street School.

Unfortunately for the rest of us, it's the TOP READER who gets to decide which book will be read in assembly. Walter is such a BIG-BOOKY-BORING-BUM-FACE! He always picks the most **<u>SNOOZIEST</u>** reads. I'm already breaking out in cold sweats and nervous rashes thinking about what awful trippy-skippy-happy-flappy story he's chosen for assembly this year.

Only a teacher would be stupid enough
to let someone as dangerously dull as
Walter pick out books for the rest of
the class to listen to.

Ugh! TEACHERS!

The terrible (T) word.

Any Menace with half a brain knows
that all adults are tricky . . . **REALLY
TRICKY** . . . but there's one kind
of adult that is more **EVIL** and
DASTARDLY than all the others . . .
EVEN WORSE THAN PARENTS!

Yep . . .

TEACHERS!

Mrs Creecher is **THE WORST** teacher in the universe. She's grumpier than a bull with a bruised bum and her favourite hobby in the world is torturing all of us at Bash Street School with tests and boring stories and . . . the dreaded  word.

The word that is even more disgusting
than the ⊤ word.

The most awful word there ever was . . .

HOMEWORK!!

Why do teachers love it so much? It's a
mystery to me . . .

If I ran Bash Street School, you can
bet that the homework would be VERY
different . . . ESPECIALLY ON WORLD
BOOK DAY! I wouldn't force my pupils to
do nightmarish things like sums and book
reports and spelling tests. **NOPE!**

I'd make everyone do BRILLIANT fun
things like . . .

A WORD SEARCH

Test your Menace level and see how many menacing words you can find.

Remember to look backwards and diagonally too!

BEANOTOWN	BUMFACE	MENACE
BELCH	CATAPULT	SOFTY
BOGEY	GNASHER	STINKBOMB

L	B	E	S	S	G	T	M	N	F
B	J	U	O	V	J	Y	E	R	T
M	M	F	M	H	S	D	N	P	L
J	T	O	F	F	C	E	A	C	U
Y	M	P	B	F	A	L	C	S	P
U	J	B	B	K	L	C	E	S	A
N	W	O	T	O	N	A	E	B	T
Y	E	G	O	B	J	I	F	X	A
G	N	A	S	H	E	R	T	V	C
Z	R	M	F	R	L	E	N	S	V

Or something to improve your secret-agent skills like . . .

SPOT THE DIFFERENCE

International Menaces of Mystery

must have sharp eyes. There are **10** differences between these two pictures. How many can you spot?

✳ Answers on page 73.

Yeah, that's what I'd do. I'd be the best teacher **EVER!** Not like all the evil ones from around the world who are behind this TERRIFYING day of flopsy—flappy—bumbly—wumbly stories. **IT HAS TO BE THEIR FAULT!** No one else would be crazy enough to invent a whole day for boring bunny books!

I can barely bring myself to think about it.

Turning **World Book Day** into a menace—tastic marvel is going to push our menacing skills to the limits, I can tell . . . Look what Headmaster gave us to take home to our mums and dads at the end of school today.

BASH STREET
SIMPER FUNGUS

Dear Parents,

It is that time of year again — World
Book Day is upon us. As always, we
will be holding lots of fun events for
the pupils here at Bash Street School.
There will be a costume parade, where
everyone will be required to dress up as
their favourite storybook character, and
each and every student will be expected
to read a short piece from their most
beloved book in class. Please see that your
child is suitably prepared for this day of
intellectual frivolity.

Sincerely,

Mr De Testa

Headmaster

YAWN!

I know what you must be thinking, my Menacing Mates. You're probably sobbing all over the pages of this diary right now, wailing, 'HOW DOES DENNIS COPE? HE'S SO BRAVE . . . HE'S A TRAGIC HERO!!' with tears and snot dripping everywhere.

Well, <u>STOP IT</u> right now!! I know it's looking like tomorrow is going to be one WHOPPING GREAT SNOOZEFEST, but things aren't hopeless just yet.

Menacing Lesson no. 77,448:
Never give up hope!
Even the most boring situations can be transformed into a menacing marvel.

If we're going to survive tomorrow and have even the tiny–teensy–weensiest scrap of fun, we've got work to do.

I've got a plan . . .

OPERATION WORLD MENACE DAY!!

First things first, my Trainee Menaces.
If old Headmaster wants us to wear
costumes to school tomorrow, we can't
let down all Menaces everywhere by
making rubbish ones.

I was going to wear my old

FRANKEN-MENACE costume

from last Halloween . . .

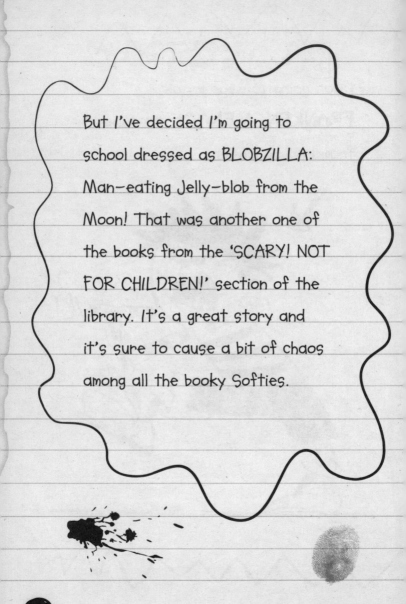

But I've decided I'm going to school dressed as BLOBZILLA: Man-eating Jelly-blob from the Moon! That was another one of the books from the 'SCARY! NOT FOR CHILDREN!' section of the library. It's a great story and it's sure to cause a bit of chaos among all the booky Softies.

BLOBZILLA
THINGS I'LL NEED

Balloons left over from my last birthday for extra-lumpy-blobbiness

Plastic fangs from Mr Har Har's Joke Shop

Pea-shooter for firing the occasional slime blob at my unsuspecting victims

Double-Bubble washing-up liquid for convincing drippy slime

You should probably have a good think about what costume you're going to wear to your school book day. Make sure you think of something super menacing.

Why don't you have a go at designing your own

MENACE-
TASTIC
costume?

Great!

Now our costumes are sorted, I can let
you in on some of my **TOP-SECRET
PLANS** for making World Book Day that
extra bit MENACING this year. I'll put
them all in this diary for you to
read and join in with . . .

But before we do that I need your
help with something. By now, all the
other Menaces around Beanotown will
be plotting just as much as me about
tomorrow. There's no way that
Minnie the Minx, Angel Face or the

Bash Street Kids will put up with another of Walter's **TERRIBLE BOOKS**.

I can always rely on them for a spot of help when a good menace is in order.

I found a menacing letter from Minnie the Minx waiting for me in my **TOP-SECRET** tree house when I got home from school.

CAN YOU HELP?

The letter is in menacing code, but me and Gnasher just haven't got time to decipher it with all our menacing plots.

THE TOP-HONKING-GREAT-
SECRET-MENACING-CODE-KEY

looks like this

Have a good look at it and never, never,

NEVER LET IT FALL INTO ENEMY HANDS!!

Can you decode it for me?

EMERGENCY MENACE MEETING

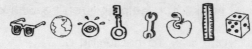

VENUE: ___ ___ ___ ___ ___ ___ ___ ___ ___

WHEN: ___ ___ ___ ___ ___ ___ ___

NO ___ ___ ___ ___ ___ ___ ___ ___

WILL BE ALLOWED IN!

✳ Answers on page 72.

BRILLIANT!

Thanks for helping. You're well on your way to becoming a

PRANKMASTER GENERAL

for certain!

Hmmm . . . sounds like there's lots of fun to be had tonight.

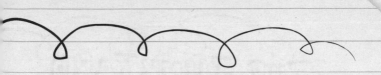

I'll just wait until Mum and Dad have finished watching their **BARGAIN BUSTERS** programme and gone to bed.

Then me and my best dog-pal, Gnasher, will sneak off to the junkyard . . .

I can't wait! The junkyard is one of the funnest places in the universe!!!

THE JUNKYARD

HIDEOUT, STOCKPILE, PLAYGROUND . . .

Some of the best HIDING PLACES in all of Beanotown

A treasure trove of MENACING SUPPLIES

What can I say? The junkyard is the

COOLEST place in the universe.

Midnight:

Wow, it looks like every Menace in town has turned up — everyone from the Bash Street Kids to my pals Curly and Pie Face and Minnie the Minx!

Even Headmaster's daughter, Angel Face, showed up! The junkyard's great. We built a TOP-SECRET den among all the rubbish here. No Softy in the world knows about it . . . **HA!**

With this many
Menaces working together,
WORLD MENACE DAY
is going to be the best day
EVER!

Right, we've got some
serious planning to do. In
the meantime, why don't you
brush up your menacing skills
even more with a few of these
BRILLIANT challenges?

DESIGN YOUR OWN
TOP-SECRET DEN

HELP DENNIS GET TO
BEANOTOWN BURGERS

Flowers + Bunnies = Softies,
so you'd better avoid them!
You don't want a Softy to follow
you to Beanotown Burgers!!

✳ Solution on page 72.

8.30 a.m.: IT'S HERE! The big day has arrived . . .

THE MENACING REVOLUTION IS UPON US! Me and the other Menaces stayed up SUPER LATE, making all sorts of MEGA plans. I can't wait for you to read about it all. Everything's here in the pages of this diary.

It's going to be a challenge though. At eight o'clock this morning, I saw Walter talking to his best snob-nosed chums, Dudley and Bertie, by his garden fence. I sneaked up behind them for a good listen and . . .

I've picked a simply SPLENDID book for today's assembly.

Then he pulled the book out of his school bag and waved it around. I nearly vomited everywhere – it was so sickly sweet!

THE ADVENTURES
OF THE
PRANCING VEGETABLE-PATCH PIXIES!!

Can you imagine!?!?

VEGETABLE-PATCH PIXIES!

It's horrible! It's unspeakable . . .

IT'S A SOFTY NIGHTMARE!!

Something has to be done or we'll be

sitting in assembly later, dying from

SUGARY-SKIPPY-OVERLOAD!

It sends shivers through my stripes . . .

I HAVE TO GET
RID OF
THAT
BOOK!

9.30 a.m.: Right! Here goes, my Menacing Mates. We're all at school and dressed in our World Book Day costumes. I look **TERRIFIC** as BLOBZILLA, even if I do say so myself.

Walter is dressed as the Magic Not-Too-Far-Away Tree . . . Ha! He has leaves and twigs in his hair and a plastic bird sitting on his arm.

WHAT A BUM-FACE!

Oh, Walter! You look TREE-MENDOUS!

Any moment now, Creecher will take us to the school hall and we'll start our World Book Day costume parade.

I'm starting to break out in a cold sweat . . .

Oh, it's not the costume parade that worries me – it's what comes afterwards. As soon as we've walked around in circles, looking like we're all completely crackers, Headmaster will make us sit on the school-hall floor and he'll . . . he'll . . . **READ US WALTER'S VEGETABLE-PATCH PIXIE BOOK!!**

I'm going to have to think on my feet for this one . . .

Menacing Lesson no. 6654:
A good Menace always thinks on their feet.
There is always a good menace to be had, even when it looks like Boredom-Brain-Rot is about to set in.

3 p.m.: Amazing! I knew this was going to be the best day EVER! And of course I thought of something . . . They don't call me **THE PRANKMASTER GENERAL** for nothing, you know.

The first thing we had to deal with was Walter's booky-boring pixie story. You should have been there, my Trainee Menaces. It was **BRILLIANT!** I'll tell you all about it . . .

Everyone was in the hall ready to start the parade and I wasn't any closer to getting my hands on Walter's book before Headmaster read it out to us. I could see it just sitting there on a table by the hall door, taunting us Menaces

with all its devious dappiness. I had to
create a distraction, but what could
I use? My costume might have been
INCREDIBLE, but it was only made up
of some plastic fangs, a load of balloons
and . . . AND . . . **DOUBLE-BUBBLE
WASHING-UP LIQUID!**

Perfect!! The plan hit me like a flash
of **GENIUS** lightning. I could see my
school bag with my copy of **Mutant
Cannibal-Zombies Ate My
Homework** in it . . . right next to
the table where Walter's book was. Then
I remembered something the Bash Street
Bandit had done at the Beanotown
Library and I knew exactly what
I had to do . . .

It went like this, my merry band of Menaces . . . I hid the bottle of soapy slime under my balloons and started squirting it all over the floor as we walked around in the parade circle. It went everywhere, but no one could tell where it was coming from. HA!

Dudley was the first person to slip. He flopped on to his face with a loud **SPLAT** and started rolling about in his sunflower costume.

Next was Bertie in his Enchanted Squirrel outfit, and then Walter with all his twigs. It was

HILARIOUS!

All three of them were slopping about, yelling and whimpering. Angel Face and Minnie even pretended to slip and fall on to the pile of Softies just for extra chaotic action.

It was **AMAZING!** The minute Headmaster saw his precious Angel Face wriggling about and screaming, he dived in to save her and I had my chance.

I bolted over to the table and grabbed

The Adventures of the Prancing Vegetable-Patch Pixies and yanked off its cover.

Then I grabbed **Mutant Cannibal-Zombies Ate My Homework** from my bag, put the pixie cover on it and placed it on the table.

I AM A MENACING
MASTERMIND!

After everyone had wriggled back to their feet and the Janitor had mopped up all the gloop, it was time for our annual story from Headmaster. Agh! I couldn't wait . . . For the first time **EVER**, it was going to be a **GREAT BOOK!** **A REALLY, REALLY GREAT BOOK!** It was going to put an end to **WORLD BORING DAY** and be the start of

WORLD MENACE DAY!

We all sat on the floor and Headmaster started to read.

And now it's time to read Walter's wonderful book, *The Adventures of the Prancing Vegetable-Patch Pixies* by Poppy Bramble-Crumpet.

It was a sunny, funny, magical type of day and the happy, smiley little boy skipped through the enchanted, breezy meadow, whistling a tune . . . WHEN A HORDE OF ZOMBIE MUTANTS BIT HIS BUM OFF! They chewed it for a minute, but then spat it out because they didn't like the taste of bum . . . so they ate his brains instead!!!!!

HA! Headmaster looked like his head was going to pop off — he was so angry! Walter sobbed all morning. For a Softy, getting detention is like being banned from eating Slopper-Gnosher-Gut-Bustin' Burgers for a month . . . AND THAT'S BAD!!

> Well, my Menacing Mates, that quickly put a stop to all the flopsy-mopsy bookiness . . .

JUST KIDDING!

Of course it isn't the end. We Menaces were only just getting started. D'you think we were going to miss the opportunity to make this the **MOST MENACING DAY IN THE HISTORY OF THE UNIVERSE EVER?** Not on your life!

Once Headmaster had stopped stomping about, muttering to himself, it was time for lunch.

Now me, Minnie, Angel Face and the Bash Street Kids have been watching Headmaster's movements for weeks, and we know that when all the pupils go to lunch in the school canteen he pops off to the teachers' loos for a quick wee and a fart in peace. Grown-ups are so weird.

Headmaster fart!

We waited until he had gone in with a copy of *Headmasters' Weekly Whinge* magazine under his arm, then we shoved one of Olive the dinner lady's brooms through the door handle . . . .

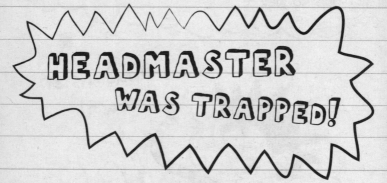

HEADMASTER WAS TRAPPED!

That was it!
THE SCHOOL WAS OURS!

Before you could say BUM—FACE,
we were in Headmaster's office and
it just so happens that I can do a
MEGA Headmaster impression. I fooled
everyone on the school PA system. I'd
never had so much fun in my life!
It's unbelievable! As long as everyone
thinks it's Headmaster talking through
the loudspeakers, they'll do whatever
he says. It was BRILLIANT!

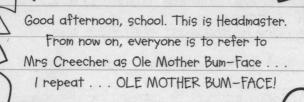

Good afternoon, school. This is Headmaster. From now on, everyone is to refer to Mrs Creecher as Ole Mother Bum-Face . . . I repeat . . . OLE MOTHER BUM-FACE!

All maths books are to be thrown away IMMEDIATELY!

No fruits or vegetables are to be eaten at lunchtime.

Walter's real name is Prince Pubert Smarmy-Pants the Seventeenth. You are to use it from now until forever. If you don't, you are a BUM-FACE!

For the next week, your homework will be completed for you by your teacher.

Instead of science, you will all attend PEA-SHOOTER accuracy classes.

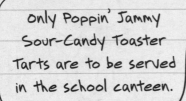

Only Poppin' Jammy Sour-Candy Toaster Tarts are to be served in the school canteen.

Home time has been changed to . . . WHENEVER YOU LIKE!

What **BRILLIANT** menacing rules can you think of? Fill in the speech bubble.

10 p.m.:

Ah! What a day . . . In just a few minutes, we turned the school into a menacing WONDERLAND! I've never seen so much chaos in the canteen . . . Mrs Creecher looked like she was about to wet herself and explode when everyone started calling her Ole Mother Bum-Face.

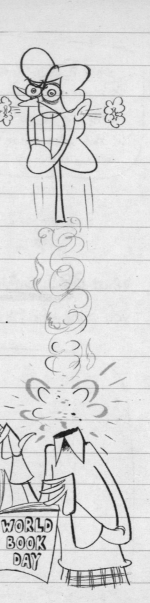

HA!

Now I'm sitting in bed with Gnasher,
enjoying a relaxing Double Fatties'
double-fat-butter-banana-
chocco-scotch sundae as a

little reward. I did invent

WORLD MENACE DAY

after all . . .

AND . . .

There's loads more menacing fun
to be had with Curly and Pie Face
tomorrow. **Life is BRILLIANT!**

I bet Headmaster was super angry

when he –

HEADMASTER!!

In all the fun and amazing, **AMAZING** menacing, I completely forgot to take the broom out from the door handle to the teachers' loos . . .

He's going to be grumpier than a baboon with bellyache when he gets out of there!

Never mind, Janitor will set him free in the morning, and . . . and . . .

I'LL JUST TELL HIM WALTER DID IT!!

Now it's time for me to settle down to read a **MEGA-BRILLIANT BOOK** with absolutely no skipping bunnies in it. Well . . . not unless they're brain-eating, mutant skipping bunnies . . .

ANswers

PAGE 15: A WORD SEARCH

L	B	E	S	S	G	T	M	N	F
B	J	U	O	V	J	Y	E	R	T
M	M	F	M	H	S	D	N	P	L
J	T	O	F	F	C	E	A	C	U
Y	M	P	B	F	A	L	C	S	P
U	J	B	B	K	L	C	E	S	A
N	W	O	T	O	N	A	E	B	T
Y	E	G	O	B	J	I	F	X	A
G	N	A	S	H	E	R	T	V	C
Z	R	M	F	R	L	E	N	S	V

PAGE 31: MENACING CODE

JUNKYARD, TONIGHT, BUM-FACES

PAGE 40: MAZE

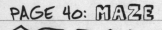

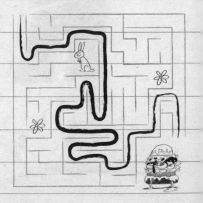

DANGERZONE BOOKS

PRESENTS

DOCTER NOEL ZONE
~Presents~

DANGER IS EVERYWHERE

with the help of my neighbours
DAVID O'DOHERTY (words)
and CHRIS JUDGE (pictures)

WARNING!
NEVER READ WHILE
CROSSING ROAD/FLYING
HELICOPTER/WRESTLING
WITH LIONS

BEWARE!
BOOK HAS
SHARP CORNERS

CAUTION!
DO NOT DROP BOOK
FROM OPEN WINDOW
(UNLESS
WEREWOLF/VAMPIRE
IS BELOW)

A HANDBOOK FOR AVOIDING DANGER

READ ON FOR SOME POTENTIALLY LIFE-SAVING TIPS . . .

FIND OUT IF YOUR TEACHER IS A VAMPIRE
OR IF YOUR DOG IS A BABY WOLF!

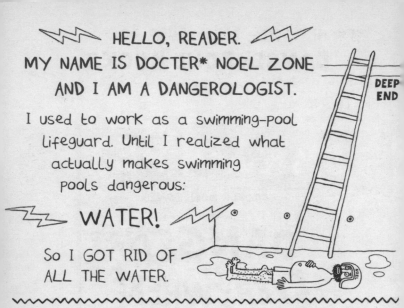

HELLO, READER.

MY NAME IS DOCTER* NOEL ZONE
AND I AM A DANGEROLOGIST.

DEEP END

I used to work as a swimming-pool
lifeguard. Until I realized what
actually makes swimming
pools dangerous:

WATER!

So I GOT RID OF
ALL THE WATER.

WHAT IS THE POINT OF MY BOOK?

That is a good question. GOOD QUESTIONING!

1. To remind you that

DANGER
~IS~
EVERYWHERE

2. To make YOU
into a qualified

DANGEROLOGIST
(Level 1)

---

* I gave myself the first name
DOCTER so I could concentrate all of
my energy on being a DANGEROLOGIST.
It saved a lot of time and hardly
anyone notices the spelling.

Here are some BSTs (Basic Safety Tips) to minimize the risk of SAHTY (Something Awful Happening To You). Thank you. DNZ.

DANGER PETS

Choosing the correct pet is a very important decision. Get it right and you have a new best friend.

Get it wrong and you have bought yourself a **ONE-WAY TICKET TO CHOMPYTOWN, IF YOU KNOW WHAT I MEAN** (what I mean is that it could eat you).

WELCOME TO

CHOMPYTOWN

POPULATION 2

(which will soon be **1** when you get chomped)

The most important question you need to ask yourself about any new pet is:

YES, IT LOOKS CUTE NOW, BUT WHAT WILL IT BE LIKE IN A YEAR?

With a new kitten, for example.

HOW CAN I BE SURE THIS CAT IS AN ORDINARY CAT AND NOT A BABY TIGER?

MEOW!

HOW TO CHECK IF YOUR CAT IS A TIGER

Ask yourself these three simple questions:

1. Is my cat much bigger than everyone else's cat?

2. Does it have very large teeth and sometimes try to eat the juiciest neighbours?

3. Instead of **MEOW**, does it go **ROAAARRRRRR** so loud that saucepans rattle and pictures on the walls go sideways?

If you answered **YES** to any **TWO** of these questions, **THEN YOUR CAT IS DEFINITELY A BABY TIGER.** You should telephone your local zoo **IMMEDIATELY.** And, while you are waiting for them to arrive, **DANCE!** (Tigers are terrified of dancing.)

IS MY DOG A BABY WOLF?

Does it **HOOOOWWWWWLL** at the moon? Does it really like chickens? Are chickens going missing in your area? Does your dog sometimes sneak out at night and have lots of feathers stuck to it in the morning and smell like chickens?

NEWSFLASH: THEN THAT IS NOT A DOG!

IS MY PET FISH A BABY GREAT WHITE SHARK?

Does it get really, really excited when you eat a sandwich in front of it? When it's hungry, does it swim along with its top fin sticking out of the water? Has it ever smashed out through its tank and eaten a member of your family?

THEN HIRE AN OLD SEA CAPTAIN/SHARK FISHERMAN TO CATCH IT BEFORE IT CHOMPS ANYONE ELSE!

Maybe you should consider getting a pet that poses NO DANGER AT ALL — what, in DANGEROLOGY, is known as an ANDAAP (Absolutely-Not-Dangerous-At-All Pet).

FOR EXAMPLE: A STONE

My pet of choice is a stone. It doesn't get hungry and you don't ever have to let it out for a pee. Add some googly eyes and take it out for a walk on a roller skate. This is my pet stone, Dennis.

I've had him for five years. He used to have a sister called Megan. But Megan got lost when I took them swimming at the beach. Dennis misses her very much. Look how sad he is, just thinking about her.

We hope to find her one day.

Dennis

Megan and Dennis

She's still somewhere out there

DANGER AT SCHOOL

IS MY TEACHER A VAMPIRE?

Vampires used to be easy to spot with their pointy capes/hair/teeth. But they realized this, and now dress much less vampirey, more like newsreaders.

A common vampire trick is to arrive at your school **POSING AS A NEW TEACHER.** 'Oh, Mr/Ms Your Normal Teacher can't come in today **(REAL REASON: AS I CHOMPED THEM),** so I will take over till they come back **(NEVER).**'

There are five ways of finding out if your new teacher is a vampire.

1. GARLIC

It is well known that vampires **HATE** garlic.
So, why not give your new teacher

A GARLICKY WELCOME GIFT?

Maybe garlic bread, or a chicken Kiev, or a
fruit basket where you have replaced all
of the fruit with bulbs of garlic.

If they run from the school screaming then

CONGRATULATIONS!

YOU HAVE SAVED EVERYONE FROM A VAMPIRE.

2. PAPER EATING

Does your teacher eat paper? I don't mean
chew on a little bit, I mean rip out pages
and stuff them into his/her mouth.

HAVE YOU EVER SEEN YOUR TEACHER FOLD UP PAGES AND PUT THEM INTO THEIR LUNCHTIME SOUP OR SANDWICH?

Well, then your teacher is
definitely a vampire. Vampires
love to eat paper. It's why
they are so pale.

3. SPARKLING WATER

Another less well-known fact about vampires is their reaction to sparkling/fizzy/bubbly water. It is not uncommon for sparkling water to make the drinker a bit burpy. But if a vampire drinks sparkling water it makes them farty.

REALLY FARTY.

Not farty like the loudest fart you've ever done though. Farty like the sound a ship makes when it is at sea and wants to say hello to another ship or a lighthouse.

HOOOONNNNK

Or when a huge truck wants to overtake another huge truck on the motorway.

HOOOONNNNK

Or when a vampire drinks sparkling water and does a fart.

HOOOONNNNK

4. A VERY EVIL LAUGH

A good way to spot a vampire is by their very evil laugh. I, like most people, laugh like this:

Ha ha ha ha.

But vampires don't laugh like that.

They laugh like this: **MWAHAHAHAHAHAHAHA.**

And they really keep going

with the **HAHAHAHAHA** part for ages.

MWAHAHAHAHAHAHAHAHAHAHAHAHAHAHA!

So try a joke out on your teacher and have a stopwatch ready.

You: Excuse me, Ms Nightstalker?

Ms Nightstalker: Yes, pupil.

You: Why did the soup have a black belt?

Ms Nightstalker: Why, pupil?

You: Because it was a carroty

(SAY IT LIKE 'KARATE') soup.

Now start timing with the stopwatch.

MWAHAHAHAHAHAHA . . .

If that laugh goes beyond ten seconds

THEN GET OUT OF THERE BECAUSE MS NIGHTSTALKER IS A VAMPIRE.

5. TURNING INTO A BAT

Finally, the best way to tell if your teacher is a vampire is if they ever turn into a bat. Vampires can't drive and generally don't get the bus, so they either travel by turning into a bat **OR BY SEGWAY.**

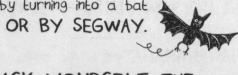

ASK YOURSELF THE FOLLOWING QUESTIONS:

A. HAVE YOU EVER SEEN YOUR TEACHER TURN INTO A BAT AT THE END OF SCHOOL?

B. DID YOUR TEACHER EVER TURN UP LATE FOR A SCHOOL AND WERE THEY A BAT?

C. DOES YOUR TEACHER COME TO SCHOOL ON A SEGWAY?

If you answered **YES** to any of these questions, **THEN YOUR TEACHER IS DEFINITELY A VAMPIRE.**

Quick, go and tell your headmaster immediately! No, wait. **FIRST MAKE SURE THAT YOUR HEADMASTER ISN'T A VAMPIRE TOO.**

WORLD BOOK DAY
5 MARCH 2015

WORLD BOOK DAY *fest*

A BIG, HAPPY, BOOKY CELEBRATION OF READING

Want to **READ** more?

VISIT your local bookshop

- Get some great recommendations for what to read next
- Meet your favourite authors & illustrators at brilliant events
- Discover books you never even knew existed!

 FIND YOUR LOCAL BOOKSHOP **www.booksellers.org.uk/bookshopsearch**

JOIN your local library

You can browse and borrow from a HUGE selection of books and get recommendations of what to read next from expert librarians—all for **FREE**! You can also discover libraries' wonderful children's and family reading activities.

 FIND YOUR LOCAL LIBRARY **www.findalibrary.co.uk**

Get ONLINE!

Visit **WORLDBOOKDAY.COM** to discover a whole new world of books!

- Downloads and activities for **FAB** books and authors
- Cool games, trailers and videos
- Author events in your area
- News, competitions and new books —all in a **FREE** monthly email

and MORE!